POOR PEPE

by

Michael Marion Sharpe

POOR PEPE

by Michael Marion Sharpe

Michele Thomas, Publisher

ACUTEBYDESIGN

Marlborough, Connecticut

https://www.acutebydesign.com

ISBN: 978-1-943515-15-8

©2019 Michael Marion Sharpe

Cover Design and Layout

T. J. WILDE

Cover Title fonts:

"RALEWAY"

by Matt McInerney

The League of Moveable Type

SIL Open Font License, Version 1.1

"DIRTY EGO"

©misprintedtype

http://www.misprintedtype.com

Cover Image Courtesy of Shutterstock.com

Dedication

Poor Pepe is a book that emerged from my heart without permission. I was a substitute teacher during the school year 2018-19 in the Springfield, MA school system. Many of my students' families were recent arrivals from Central America. Some spoke English; others did not.

I saw in their faces the same love and happiness, fear and sadness that I have seen in the faces of my African American children.

One of my fond memories was the day I took the kids out for recess, in my mind to play the all-American game, kickball. I rolled the ball to the first kicker, who properly kicked the ball, but then he and all the players chased after the ball, repeatedly kicking it with their feet.

I was horrified; I blew the whistle for them to stop. "What are you doing?" I demanded to know.

One little boy said, "Mister! We don't understand your rules. This is how we play soccer."

"But this is kickball!" I insisted.
This started a long argument with the alpha boys in the class. A very tiny African American girl pulled at my sleeve and said, "Mister! Let's just play soccer. We are running out of time!"

I dedicate this book to that African American girl and all first-generation Latino children, refugees, and immigrants, who understand that we must learn to play together because recess time is running out!

~ MMS

Acknowledgments

There were many early critical readers who, without mercy, unabashedly shared their opinions: Michele Thomas, executive publisher, AbyD; Shawn Thomas, perennial supporter; Cynthia MacGregor, AbyD editor and author of 100-plus books; Michael Murray, mentor for young boys and alleged master fisherman. Cathy Saunders, dearest friend, and honorary family member since forever; Patricia O'Hearn-Berger, high school classmate and a brilliant retired educator. Cory Hills, master percussionist, author and all-around cool guy; Cynthia Belton, classmate Columbia-Barnard University, a brilliant mind, and beautiful human being. Ava Mercurius, who sent an encouraging review at a time when I was most discouraged; and Kenya Washington, the soul of a poet, and lover of humankind.

Poor Pepe was a work of love, and I thank all my family, friends and strangers who helped me along the way.
-MMS

Prologue

Over the years, those granted hardship admission into the United States more easily acquired social, political, and economic wealth. Meanwhile, others, who entered the country illegally, became shadow citizens, working as undocumented farm hands, hotel staff, housecleaners and lawn-care maintenance workers, non-citizens but in every other way living as Americans. They became the illegals, the undocumented, the DREAMers!

There is a price paid by undocumented children. Some succumb to the bleak gray uncertainty of not existing, while others emerge victoriously, but at what cost?

This is Pepe's story: the emotional struggle of a boy who lives with his mother in a wealthy Hispanic community. Its families were wealthy. His was not! They were documented. His was not!

Pepe lived 50 miles east of the blue Pacific Ocean and 150 miles from the infamous wall that paranoia built to separate the two worlds of South America and the United States. He lived in a small, affluent American-Latino town, populated by second- and third-generation Latinos who had made it in America.

It was not always so; for decades, and to this day, human caravans heading north from Honduras, El Salvador, Guatemala and many other South American countries traveled thousands of dangerous miles, facing starvation, robbery, rape and death toward Mexico to find sanctuary in America. Many thousands of those travelers were and are children traveling alone.

Chapter 1

I thought life would be warm and inviting,
but instead it is creepy and sinister!

Maria Colon, a skinny fourteen-year-old from Guatemala, was one of the thousands of unaccompanied minors traveling with the largest South American caravan ever to wind its way toward the United States. She sat next to a grieving mother from Honduras who had recently lost her daughter to a kidnapping. The mother could not turn back. Like most migrants on this caravan, she had given up everything to make this journey to a new life. The mother did not have the strength to return home, nor the power to avenge the assault upon her twelve-year-old child. So, she stared at nothing as she tightly held the hand of this young girl she did not know. Maria did not mind lending her hand to this grieving lady but thought she would never release her grip.

The caravans of migrants did not go unnoticed in the United States. The president of the United States had recently tweeted his decision to declare a state of emergency and order American armed forces to the border. He claimed, without proof, that the United States was being invaded by tens of thousands of murderers, violent gang members belonging to the MS-12 and migrants and refugees who were among the worst of Central America's citizens.

His words were greeted as racist and untrue by leaders of the opposing political party and socially liberal Americans: "Shame! Shame, on you, Mr. President."

The president scoffed at the protesters with a raw indifference. He was supported by the thirty-three percent of Americans who thought he could do no wrong. The president ordered 5000 military troops to the border. The armed soldiers and state and national guards stood alert and ready to follow the orders of their commander-in-chief, the president of the United States.

The American Civil Liberties Union immediately filed a cease-and-desist action, claiming the president was in violation of the Posse Comitatus Act, which forbids the use of federal troops to enforce domestic law.

Frightened, young Maria clutched her bright pink denim jacket with her free hand and peered from her bus window. She did not understand the Posse Comitatus Act or even the requirements necessary to be granted asylum. She knew only that she was tired, sweaty, unwashed and badly in need of something to eat—and this grieving lady sitting beside her would not turn her hand loose.

The bus was alive with passengers laughing at a man's stand-up comedy of crude jokes. A group of women and children competed for the bus's attention singing "La Cucaracha," one of Latin America's iconic but controversial traditional folk melodies. This had been a long trip of several months and more for some. Singing, joking and sleeping were the only forms of daily entertainment.

On Maria's bus, the festive mood had slowly simmered as passengers sensed something afoot. The vehicle had slowed, and their leaders huddled behind the bus driver, conferring in whispers. A voluntary hush overtook the bus as the caravan pulled within sight of their destination: the Hidalgo-Reynosa bridge at the San Ysidro port of entry.

No one spoke! Only silence could voice the words of the

2

anxious faces pressed close to the glass windows as if proximity would answer all their questions. The port of entry loomed near; its powerful floodlights illuminated every corner of earth within its jurisdiction. Mexican military patrol units powered by Hummer-like vehicles stood watch over the Mexican territory, daring anyone to make a wayward move. High caliber machine guns pointed outward from custom-made combat windows reinforced the stern warning of the military *policia*.

Maria was surprised! She had thought the port of entry would be warm and inviting. Instead, the Hidalgo-Reynosa Bridge loomed creepy and sinister; its metal gates, concrete blocks, and barbed-wire fencing gave it a look of being impenetrable. It was not at all welcoming. The bridge seemed but a few feet from their bus, perhaps a strong rock's throw. It might as well have been a thousand miles away; few in this caravan would ever cross that bridge and make it to the American side.

Jose and the other leaders on the bus knew the real battle was only now beginning. The caravan of buses and vans pulled to the roadside to wait. The driver turned the ignition switch to Off. The abrupt quiet of the formerly loud diesel engine only added to the silence on the bus. Jose kneeled and prayed, and several other asylum-seekers joined him.

Ironically, Maria's caravan arrived at the border the day after the United States District Court, Southern District of California ruled that the president was in violation of the Posse Comitatus Act and ordered the soldiers removed from the borders.

An angry and defiant president was briefed on the court ruling, but he misunderstood several vital facts. He tweeted a directive to his military leaders based on his misunderstanding, and they then cabled an incorrect directive to their ground command to remove all military personnel from the border.

The combined misunderstandings confused the Secretary of Homeland Security, who then issued an unclear order that left the port of entry protected by only a few dozen border and Customs officers. This series of miscommunications was later described as the biggest cluster F.U. in modern military-political history.

The following day, the leaders of the caravan walked to the port of entry, followed by hundreds of refugees and asylum-seekers. They were stopped at the entrance by border agents and ordered to turn around.

Maria listened as Jose spoke through a bullhorn-loud speaker so that all could hear. "We are seeking protection under the asylum laws of the United States." Jose pointed to the hundreds of people behind him. "These people have arrived at your port of entry, fleeing from persecution and death because of their race, religion and social-political beliefs. Please allow us entry."

Maria heard the words "people who are seeking safety from persecution and harm." She began to have a glimmer as to what was meant by asylum.

Border security officers stood firm and told Jose that there was insufficient staff on duty to process their claims and to come back the next day. Jose and the caravan people retreated and peacefully returned the next day with the same request. They were again rebuffed and told to return the next day. This continued for several more days in a row.

The people were hot, thirsty, hungry and becoming increasingly agitated. The sanitary conditions were horrific. There was nowhere to wash their bodies or to care for general hygiene. Children were falling ill by the dozens. The crowd began to call for more direct action. Shouts to storm the gate started to resonate with the crowd. Jose's calls for calm rang hollow as the people scrunched together, one on top of the other, began pushing and inching toward the gate.

No leader gave the command. No asylum seeker said, "Charge!" It was the spontaneous explosion of nuclear-like energy radiating the anger and frustration of poor and oppressed people who only wanted a better life. Maria had no understanding of what was happening! She was pulled along with the crowd as they exploded toward the gate.

The guards at the port of entry point had stood nervous for several days and nights, knowing that they had no backup protection. Homeland Security told the officers to stand firm; the problem was being worked out in Washington. There was no advance intelligence that the migrants were going to rush the gates. In fact, Jose and the other leaders had assured border patrol that it would not happen.

But it did. The people charged the gate; the border patrol officers were caught flat-footed. The officer in charge placed an emergency call to the Homeland Security office in Washington. He was asked if he could hold.

"Are you shitting me? We are under attack! We need help! *Now!*" the officer screamed into the phone.

A classic bureaucratic voice came on the phone, "Hi Bob—this is Bob, correct? This is the assistant undersecretary. How can we help you down there?"

"Get help down here now. This is a f-ing May Day! They are storming the bloody freaking gates!" The border-Customs officer slammed the phone down and ran to give support to his team. They were being overwhelmed at the gate.

Within minutes of the May Day call, the secretary of Homeland Security authorized the border officers to use deadly force. A bloody battle unfolded as the border patrol attempted to fight back the angry asylum-seekers.

Chapter 2

Your actual wealth is determined by how you value your world!

Pepe sat on the brick stoop of his old red brick six-family home. Looking left, he saw the immaculate mansions and pristine swimming pools of the *afluente*; stately homes decorated the hillsides, giving proof to the slogan, "America, the land of opportunity." It was little comfort to Pepe; as he looked to the right from his stoop, he saw the mega-rich downtown, called the Valley: exclusive boutiques, surrounded by intricate iron fencing and formidable entrances that proclaimed, *los ricos solamente*—for the rich only.

Beyond the super-rich stores were the town's elite schools, rated the best learning centers in all the state. Spit-polished yellow school buses proudly purred to a stop, pouring out their wealthy well-appointed students. The little Fauntleroys congregated at the entrance, shiny new leather shoes, pressed gray pants, bright blue blazers, emblems stitched above their hearts proclaimed their economic pedigree.

To drive from the wealthy hills or to the prosperous downtown, you had to pass Pepe's home. His old red brick, six-family building stood as the iconic gateway between these two points of wealth. Pepe named his home "*Casa de la pobreza*, the house of poverty!"

His old red brick building was not much to look at. There were six apartments, one on each floor. There was no elevator, so each day Pepe climbed up and down the six flights of stairs gripping the worn mahogany banisters. The stairway was old and creaky but strong, clean, and never was there a hint of debris anywhere. His mother would never permit it. Pepe and *su madre's* tenants knew this.

The outside was as clean as the building's inside, and the stoop was swept each day and washed twice a week. The small yard, facing Main Street, was mostly red brick, with a patch of grass running along a short, white picket fence. A few plants bordered the roadside. All the tenants took care that no harm should come to these plants. Nobody knew their names, and no flower ever sprouted on them, but they were green and vibrant living things, and they were *su madre's* pride and joy!

Across the street, from his home, a colorful blue sign announced BUS STOP. It was the only bus stop before reaching the wealthy rolling hills or the affluent downtown. "No doubt," thought Pepe, "placed there to accommodate *mi madre*," who rode the bus every morning to clean the homes of the wealthy homeowners. It might as well have said "POVERTY STOP."

Pepe had two important responsibilities. He helped his mother each morning down the six flights of stairs, out the door, down the stoop and across the street to catch her bus to work. She carried cleaning equipment, sprays, scrapers, rags and odds and ends that she used to make the wealthy hillside homes immaculately clean.

When Pepe arrived home from school, he waited on the stoop for his mother's bus. As he sat there on the stoop, the rich people on their way home to their mansions drove past his old red brick apartment building; some beeped their horns and gave a friendly wave at Pepe. It was a small town, and everyone knew of each other. But Pepe ignored them. He was ashamed of where he lived. He kept his gaze on his book and didn't look up at the sound of the friendly horns. He was embarrassed to be seen in front of his *casa de* poverty.

Pepe didn't share his feelings with his mother. As much as he loved her—and he loved her very much—he resented the fact that they lived as they did. Why didn't they have more money? Why did she have to work cleaning houses? And why didn't he have a father? His mother never talked about his father.

Pepe's mother would soon arrive home. Stepping off the bus, she looked toward Pepe with a big smile! She would wave and call out, "Pepe, my love, I'm home."

Pepe looked away! She wore an old, faded, calico flowered dress that hardly fit her properly and shoes that looked a size too big. He was embarrassed! Pepe wondered why she could not wear a nice dress and new shoes and drive a fancy car like the wealthy families from the hills. But as she approached, Pepe's heart would melt, and he wanted nothing more than to relieve her burden. He hugged *su madre* despite his regrets and helped with her bags.

Chapter 3

Poverty is as poverty does.

Another irony did not escape Pepe. He, too, was
expected to catch the bus—the school bus, in his case—directly
in front of his *casa de* poverty. Pepe would not make eye
contact with the other children. He sensed the rich kids were
peering through the school bus windows looking at his home.
He was certain that, as he moved to the back of the bus, they
were snickering at him as well. He never looked up at the other
children.

For many years, Pepe's mom thought that he was just
shy. Pepe's teachers told his mother how he sat by himself at
lunchtime, walked quietly in the hallways without talking to
anyone, and seldom interacted with his classmates. But the
teachers allowed this odd behavior because Pepe was such an
excellent, well-behaved student. "Of course, he will grow out of
it," they promised his mother. But Pepe did not grow out of it.
Pepe didn't look others in the eyes or play with his classmates
when he was younger, or socialize with them as he became older.
He kept to himself and didn't make friends with any of the others
because for years he felt in his heart—well, that he was not
worthy.

Pepe's fourth-grade teacher, Ms. LaFleur, argued, "There
is nothing normal about his behavior. Ms. LaFleur insisted
that the school hold a student-assessment hearing to determine
whether Pepe needed special services. Her perseverance finally
paid off.

An early morning meeting in the principal's office was arranged to accommodate Maria Colon's work schedule. Ms. LaFleur arrived holding a stack of reports and teacher assessments that she had collected on Pepe.

Su madre arrived promptly at seven am, followed by Mr. Casio, the school principal, and Mr. Sanchez, the social worker. Ms. Colon's ability to arrive precisely at the designated time of school meetings was jokingly referred to as the "Eighth Wonder of the World." She caught the bus everywhere she went about town, but still she was one of the few people always on time. This particular meeting did not go at all as Maria Colon had thought it would.

After introductions, Ms. LaFleur started the conversation. "Pepe's lack of social skills greatly concerns me. According to his student records, his refusal to socialize with the other students or participate in group activities has been going on since his kindergarten years. I am concerned that this behavior could be indicative of a more serious problem. I think we should consider a battery of psychological tests so that we can find the core cause and develop a plan of action."

Mr. Sanchez immediately interrupted. "Typical! Every time one of our children has a perceived issue, the immediate response by some of you people is to test, label and put the child in special education. I don't think testing is needed at this time. He is an excellent student and very well behaved. If I were Pepe, I wouldn't socialize with some of these students either," joked Mr. Sanchez.

Ms. LaFleur did not appreciate the joke. She stood, trembling in anger. "I resent your comment: 'You people'! Who the hell is 'you people'? I care about Pepe and all our students, just as much as you or anyone else. I am not defined by my being white!"

The principal interrupted. "Now, Ms. LaFleur, please sit down. I am certain that Mr. Sanchez did not make his comments to be offensive or as a personal attack against you."

"Then what were they?" Ms. LaFleur demanded to know as she sat down.

Pepe's mother was confused as dozens of questions raced through her mind, all in Spanish. "What was all this talk about testing and special education? Why are they talking about his teacher being white? What does that have to do with anything? What does Pepe being well behaved have to do with his shyness in talking with his classmates?" But she did not ask any of those questions. She respectfully listened to the experts.

The heated discussion was ended when the principal said, "I agree with Mr. Sanchez. Let's keep an eye on Pepe and see what happens. I do not think an intervention is needed at this time. I believe he will grow out of this behavior."

Ms. LaFleur abruptly stood. "Another child left to figure it out on his own. This is criminal!" and she stormed from the room.

Pepe's mom sensed that what had happened in that meeting was unacceptable and somehow not in her son's best interest. But what did she know? They were the experts. She accepted the principal's decision without challenge.

Pepe continued to read alone during recess and seldom talked to or played games with the other students. One girl, named Julia, would often sit next to Pepe. This made Pepe uncomfortable at first, but he soon came to enjoy her quiet presence. She did not try to talk to him, but she was always close by to defend Pepe. When the class had to find project partners, it seemed Julia and Pepe gravitated to each other.

Chapter 4

Running Away! Running Toward!
It's all the same if you don't know where you are running!

Somewhere during the second or third grade, Pepe decided he no longer wanted the school bus to stop in front of his house. He hated walking past the other students as he walked to the back of the bus, although where he sat was his choice.

While the other boys and girls used the time on the bus to chat, complain about the school lunch, or discuss the NBA standings, Pepe studied. He would place his backpack next to him on an empty seat, take out a textbook or chapter book and read.

He was always relieved when the school bus pulled away from the bus stop in front of his house. His old red brick apartment building was not much to look at. It was not a private house like his classmates all lived in. Why couldn't he live in a beautiful big house like so many of the other children?

Pepe didn't tell his mother of his plan, but one day he decided to stop taking the bus, and instead he started running to school. The running distance from Pepe's home to school was five miles. He jogged past the fancy store windows displaying Rolex watches, Armani suits, and Louis Vuitton handbags. Farther along, he became fascinated by the shiny, sleek cars parked along the roadway: BMWs, MBZs, Maseratis and Ferraris. He dreamed that one day he would own a fire engine red Ferrari-812.

The downtown faded to his back, but he still had miles to go. His chest started to ache, and his breathing became labored. Pepe began to think maybe this wasn't such a smart idea after all.

Pepe arrived at school, and he stood in the hallway bending over in pain and gasping for breath. His clothes were wet from sweat. Julia ran to inform the homeroom teacher that Pepe was sick in the hallway. The teacher, on seeing Pepe, immediately sent him to see Mr. Gavel, the school nurse.

After Pepe explained to the nurse why he was wet, sweaty and breathing hard, Mr. Gavel let out a deep belly laugh. "You've got a lot of guts to run five miles to school at your age." The nurse gave Pepe a clean sweatpant and top and then sent him back to class. Pepe sat at his desk and swore he would never do that again. He was going to ride the bus home.

By afternoon he had caught his second wind, however, and instead of riding the school bus, he raced by foot to his home. He thought he was moving briskly, but it was getting late, and he was still not close to home. In fact, he had yet to reach downtown. He realized that he would be late meeting his mother, and that was not acceptable. *Su madre* was going to be angry with him.

Tears began to well in his eyes and roll down onto his sweaty, tired face. He had only two responsibilities: to help his mother to and from the bus stop. Pepe tried to run faster; his lungs only burned hotter while his legs churned slower. His body refused to respond to his brain's command, "Go faster."

Su madre sat on the stoop, very upset. Pepe was the only family she had in the world. She began to worry aloud to herself. "What if he was in an accident? No! Please no," she moaned. She quickly allayed her fear, saying, "They would have come to me by now. No?"

A horrific thought came to mind: What if the government had picked up Pepe. She had hidden her illegal status from him. Why had she done that, she chastised herself? *I should have told him so that he could protect himself.* *Su madre* allowed her fears to control her thoughts. "Nothing can happen to Pepe. I have endured so much for us to be a part of this country."

****

Maria was one of the hundreds of migrants who had rushed the gates at the San Ysidro port of entry. It was only later that she learned twenty people had been killed that early morning. Jose pushed her to the ground as gunfire erupted. A bullet tore into his chest. She remembered the gushing red blood and his eyes fluttering as he whispered to her, "*¡Levántate y corre!* Get up and run! Don't stop until you are safe."

Maria stood and ran! It was total confusion as hundreds of men and women pushed past her. Parents were screaming for their separated children as unclaimed children stood alone, screaming for their parents. The border patrol was now randomly shooting their guns, trying to regain control of the gate by the sheer power of their weapons.

Maria was knocked to the ground. She tried to stand, but the retreating crowd and advancing patrol officers knocked her small body back to the pavement. She curled into a ball as hundreds of feet trampled on or near her. It seemed hours before the area cleared, but it was just a few minutes. There was the occasional wailing of a nearby injured person. Maria could still hear gunshots in the distance.

Maria lay on the ground, sobbing, stunned but not seriously hurt. A lone woman was running toward the American border while stepping over fallen bodies. Her direction was opposite from that of the retreating crowd. She moved toward the American border. The lone lady as she stepped over a small body recognized the pink denim jacket. It was the little girl from the bus who had sat patiently, allowing the grieving mother to squeeze her hand. . The lady grabbed Maria's hand and tried to yank her afoot. Maria resisted. The grieving mother yelled, "*¡Levántate y corre!* Get up and run!" It was the woman who had gripped Maria's hand on the bus. Maria stood and ran.

Maria Colon forced herself to forget most of what happened on that journey and that night outside the San Ysidro port of entry. However, she would always remember Jose, as he died urging her, "*¡Levántate y corre!* Get up and run!"

Maria would also never forget the grieving mother who slowed to pull her to safety. She would forever remember feeling hope and protection as she ran past a red, white and blue sign that read: *¡Bienvenido a América!* Welcome to America!

****

Pepe rounded the corner, and there sat his mother on the stoop, surrounded by her cleaning bags of odds and ends. Her head hung low, held in place by the upturned palms of her two hands. She was sobbing.

Pepe's heart dropped toward the empty pit in his stomach. Reaching *su madre*, Pepe cried out, "*¡Lo siento!* I am so sorry, mamá!" His mother looked up, and on seeing Pepe, she embraced him tightly and kissed him several times on his forehead.

"*Mijo*, I was so worried for you," exclaimed his mother. Relief spread across her face. She wiped at her eyes with the back of her hand. She continued, "I thought something terrible had happened to you. You have never missed meeting me since you started school."

It was not the reaction Pepe had expected. He had thought she would be angry. He would have preferred her anger over seeing her in tears. In his mind, Pepe begged his mother, "Hit me! Punish me. Yell at me! Please do not cry."

But aloud, he said to his mother the one dumb thing that would make her angrier: "*Mamacita*, why are you crying? I am only a few minutes late."

She shook him by his shoulders. "Pepe, do not scare me like this again," she yelled. "You must ride the bus! *Comprende?*"

"*Madre!* I do not wish to ride the school bus any longer. I don't like the way the other kids look at me. I don't like the way they look at our home," pouted Pepe.

"Pepe!" admonished *su madre*, "How can you know how they look at you if you never look up to see them? You are acting like poor Pepe once again. The children on the bus adore you.

20

It is you who does not like Pepe. You think the world is against you," scolded *su madre*! "You do not appreciate all that you have because you spend your days being jealous of what others have. Poor Pepe!"

Pepe cringed. He hated it when his mother called him "poor Pepe!" "You just don't understand!" he cried.

Su madre's beautiful dark Latina eyes flashed her anger, "*Bastante!* Enough! Your behavior is foolishness. I don't care whether you ride the bus, take a train or fly a plane!" *su madre* warned, paraphrasing her favorite Oleta James song, "but you had better be here when I arrive home from work." Pepe and *su madre* did not speak as they walked the six flights of stairs.

Pepe awoke early the next morning. He lay on his bed, listening to the familiar house sounds—his mother clanging pots, and opening and closing the cupboards—and inhaled the pleasant aroma of eggs and turkey bacon. Pepe wondered if he should catch the bus or run to school? The answer came quickly. Pepe jumped from his bed, showered, ate breakfast, and began to implore his mother to hurry. She was going to make him late.

Pepe rushed *su madre* to the bus stop, waving as her bus pulled from the curb. He then turned toward his school and the affluent downtown and began to run, faster and stronger than the day before. Pepe was a very determined boy!

At the day's end, Pepe raced home on foot, determined not to make his mother wait. As he rounded the corner, his mother's bus was arriving. *Su madre* looked out the bus window and saw Pepe running toward her. She smiled! Pepe smiled!

Pepe ran to and from school every day, week, month, and year until his senior year in high school. He was never late again.

Chapter 5

Surface discords often hide the underlying
sounds of harmonic unison!

There was something else that bugged Pepe. The five
tenants in la casa de poverty. They all played their instruments
alone in their apartments but at the same time every evening. It
was hard to hear the noise from Pepe's apartment, but once he
walked out into the hallway, what an awful racket he heard!

It was an un-orchestrated blaring of 1000 car horns,
the roar of 100 jet engines and the high-pitched screaming of
kindergarteners at recess. His neighbors had to be the worst
musicians in the world!

On the first floor was Teddy, the percussionist. He
crashed his cymbals and made unworldly thumping sounds on
his conga drums, all seemingly without tempo or purpose.

Al-Raul, on the second floor, was worse. His monotone
solos on his saxophone raised the question of why God had
created such an instrument.

Juanita, on the third floor, was a singer. She screeched
high and low notes all evening, long spews of unidentifiable
melodies. The fourth and fifth floors were no better than the first,
second and third floors. They were all, in Pepe's mind, wanna-be
musicians crumbling the foundation on which stood the old red
brick, six-family apartment building.

The five musicians had been feuding for years, but not
one of them remembered why! They passed in the hallway but

would not speak to each other. Pepe complained to his mother about the so-called musicians. She would only smile and say, "Be kind, Pepe! Everyone has bad and good days in this life— maybe just not on your schedule."

Madre was one of the few people who knew the story behind the musicians falling apart and how they all came to live in her apartment house. Most Valley residents dismissed them as five eccentric musicians who all happened to live in the same building.

They had been the best of friends, like family. Together, they traveled all over South America and the Caribbean, playing at famous clubs, hotels and resorts. They vacationed together, and each took care of the other. While on tour in Cuba, one of their members was killed in a night club outside of Havana. The grief and guilt of the remaining members were unbearable. The close-knit band-family gradually fell apart as each wallowed in their personal grief. During bouts of drinking, they often blamed each other for their fellow band member's death.
This unhealthy way of dealing with their pain continued for a very long time. One day—and no one remembers why—they just stopped talking to each other.

Several years ago, a very flamboyant and wealthy member of the Valley invited the Caribbean All-Stars to play at his daughter 15th birthday party, her *quinceañera*. He promised to pay them at the end of their gig. Maria Colon was hired as one of the servers at the party. The party was billed as the Mother of all *Quinceañeras*.

As the guest arrived, one disaster led to another. The Caribbean All-Stars were all drunk. The father, who had paid a small fortune to ensure his daughter had the best quinceañera ever, was furious. He had a wooden baseball bat in hand and was moving toward the band, no doubt to give them a beating within an inch of their lives.

At that moment the front and back doors crashed in, followed by dozens of FBI agents, yelling "FBI, no one move." Of course, on this command to be still, all of the guests, parents and children rushed for windows, doors and any other opening allowing them exit. The flamboyant dad was arrested and whisked away in a black SUV with dark, tinted windows. The house had emptied out except for Maria Colon and the five now-sober band members.

The Caribbean All-Stars had not been paid, and they had no money to get out of the Valley. Maria heard the band talking, saying that they had nowhere to stay and no money in their pockets until their monthly royalty checks from their former recordings were deposited in their bank accounts.

Maria saw the silver lining in this disaster of a day! She had just purchased her six-family building and was struggling to find renters. She offered to rent the five band members one of her apartments as long as they paid her when their checks arrived. The band members insisted that they each needed their own apartment. They each promised to pay her at the end of the month. Maria was desperate for income, so she agreed. That had been many years ago. The Caribbean All-Stars never left her apartment house.

The years rolled by quickly. This was to be Pepe's life. He helped his mother each day down and up the stoop and the stairs. He ran to and from school, each day faster than the day before, and he listened to the blaring noise of the five musicians without knowing their backstory. Pepe studied hard, and his school grades got better and better; even so, he would not look the townspeople or his classmates in the eyes. Yet, no one said anything! *Su madre* loved him deeply, but she only said, "poor Pepe."

Chapter 6

Every season has an end that leads to a beginning.

The years rolled on. Finally it was late August, and the next day Pepe was to start his senior year of high school. My, how Pepe had grown. He stood a muscular six feet tall and was broad-shouldered, with thick black curly hair that crowned his caramel brown face. Still-water deep, dark brown eyes mirrored his mother's eyes, flashing love and anger with equal effect. He was a very handsome boy!

But this senior year was not to be anything like his past twelve years. In two weeks, Pepe would be seventeen years of age. "Pepe! I am having a birthday party for you." *Su madre* looked toward her son, awaiting the outburst she knew would come.

Right on cue, Pepe yelled, "No way! Absolutely not!"

"I've invited all your classmates!" *Su madre* egged him on.

Pepe was horrified! "Have the party where?" he asked. "Not here! The kids will not come to this house!"

"Enough! You have prevented me from having parties for you all your school life. This is your last school year, and I am having a party for you. It's done! The invitations have been delivered. Go! Do your school work or whatever it is you do! See if you can get a scholarship to some community college," his mother jabbed at him.

It was certain that Pepe would be class valedictorian and should be able to attend one of the great universities. He quietly worried that "something about his documents" might prevent him from attending any school but a community college. Pepe glared at his mother. He knew she was joking, but it hurt nonetheless. She knew he wanted to be a lawyer and had applied for early admission to Columbia University.

"Fat chance!" snapped Pepe. "How could I become anything important attending a community college?"

Pepe's outbursts did not dissuade *su madre*; she continued with her plans to host a seventeenth birthday party for Pepe.

The next day Pepe started school. The day started as it had every year since forever, it seemed. He helped his mother down the stairs and onto the bus before he raced off to school. Pepe had been running the five miles to school since second or third grade.

On this particular morning, Coach Steve Harris had taken a different route to work. As he neared the downtown area a few miles from the high school, he drove past a student running toward Valley High. The student had a heavy-looking bookbag on his shoulder that appeared to be full of books. Yet he was sprinting toward the school in full stride. Coach smiled, thinking, "He will never make it to school in time."

Coach glanced at his watch, "Oh damn! It's seven-fifty. I'm going to be late myself!" Coach Harris arrived at school three minutes later, greeted a few students in the parking lot and then headed inside the school building. A student held the door for him. Coach Harris's mouth fell open. It was the runner from downtown. It was now 7:57 am. This student had run three miles from downtown with a bookbag on his back in seven minutes.

"That's not possible," the coach muttered to himself. "He must have gotten a ride! No way! Yo! Yo! Excuse me!" the coach called after Pepe.

Surprised, Pepe turned with a puzzled expression as if to ask, "You talking to me?"

"Yes, you! Did you run all the way to school from downtown?"

Pepe avoided the coach's eyes, but he answered, "I run to and from school every day."

"You live in the old Victorian right outside of town?" asked Coach Harris.

There it was, thought Pepe. "It always comes back to where I live and how poor
I am."

Coach looked at Pepe incredulously. You are the best runner I have ever seen in my twenty years of coaching! I want you on my track team."

Pepe laughed nervously. "I've never run track in my life," he said, and he continued walking toward class.

Coach was not one to take no for an answer. He realized from watching Pepe run that he had witnessed a talent that might show itself once in a lifetime. But Pepe would not give him the time of day. "Son," explained Coach, "your talent is a gift from God. You must run."

Pepe shyly smiled and said, "I am going to college. I need to study. I do not have time for sports."

Coach visited Pepe's teacher-advisor, who was not hopeful, but she did agree to talk with Pepe and his mom. The advisor thought a team sport might be just the thing for Pepe. She convinced Maria Colon and Pepe to give it a try, explaining that colleges like to see their student applicants not only have good grades but also have participated in extracurricular activities. Pepe and his mother agreed to give it a try.

30

Chapter 7

Have fun, but never let anyone get in front of you!

And there it was! Pepe was a member of the track team. He did not have time to train like the other runners. By the time he joined the team, their first track meet was two days away. Pepe was devastated; he could never train to run in that short time! The other runners looked at Pepe with suspicion, which was not at all unusual. Most new athletes on an existing team are viewed with suspicion and apprehension until they prove themselves.

The Valley track team members were surprised to see a new guy on their team two days before the season was to start. They had been in training for months in preparation for their first track meet; this guy has never trained. In fact, he did not even have running shoes; he wore street sneakers. A worry spread through the locker room that Coach was losing his edge.

Pepe viewed their suspicions not as valid concerns but as proof of his lifelong belief that the Valley kids did not accept him. Pepe thought of quitting, but Coach wouldn't hear of it.

Coach Harris showed him how to follow the cross-country trail markings and warned him that if he did not follow the trail, he would be disqualified; still, Pepe kept getting lost.

This kid couldn't even follow the colored flag-markers on the trees, his teammates worried. "Coach is going to get us disqualified." Such are the worries inherent in the locker room of any sports team.

That afternoon, Pepe's teammates got to run against him in a practice mile run. At the crack of the starter's gun, Pepe jumped from the starter's line with the power of a panther. His strides were long and unrelenting. Before Pepe turned the bend toward the half-mile mark, he was far in front of his teammates. Coach smiled, watching from the sidelines. He was sure that Pepe was showing off.

The experienced runners could not keep pace. As they crossed the mile finish line, sweating and breathing hard, Pepe stood on the sidelines talking with the coach. Pepe was not breathing hard, and he certainly was not sweating. The most skeptical of his teammates knew that he was something special. The teammates extended the olive branch.

"Nice job, Pepe! You looked really good out there," acknowledged the team captain.

The other members shook his hand and slapped him on the back. "Good going!"

Pepe glanced up at the team captain, almost looking him in the eyes before lowering his head, and said, "Thank you."

Coach called Pepe into his office. "Pepe, I have only two rules; follow them, and you will do fine! First, just have fun! Second, never let another runner get in front of you!"

Shifting nervously from foot to foot, Pepe repeated, "So, all I have to do is have fun and keep all the other runners behind me?" Pepe could not resist a quick glance into Coach's face. Pepe saw the mischief twinkling in Coach's eyes; they both began to laugh. It felt good. It was the first time Pepe had become a part of something at school without thinking about his poverty.

"Maybe joining a team activity wasn't such a bad idea after all," thought Pepe. It was nice looking into Coach's eyes.

The day of the track meet came quickly. Coach Harris

gave Pepe a pair of used cross-country sneakers and an old running uniform he pulled out of a musty box. Pepe nervously dressed and then walked out to the track and cross-country trail with Coach.

Pepe was impressed! The other team had just arrived in a blue and white limo bus, their school name emblazoned across its midsection. It cruised to a graceful stop and sat undisturbed for a few minutes before the driver pulled open its door. Their coach came to the door, dapper plus in his Giorgio Armani three-piece suit. He stood tall in the bus doorway, his Cartier Aviator shades sweeping the field before focusing on a man moving in his direction.

Valley's coach moved toward the blue limo-bus in long official strides. The psychological warfare between the opposing coaches was in full gear. The blue team's coach only then stepped down from the bus and shook hands with Valley's coach. After this official greeting ritual between the coaches, the forty members of the elite track team stepped from the bus, all wearing custom-made royal blue jerseys with their name and a number stitched on the back.

Dozens of Valley teachers and administrators milled about the field, shaking hands and glancing about to ensure they were seen. Boisterous students, sporting the gold and crimson school colors of Valley High, cheered and yelled from the nearby bleachers. Several official-like students walked about with clipboards writing important things on pieces of paper.

The runners were on the grass, stretching and doing short warm-up sprints in preparation for the many events, which included the classic hundred-yard dash, pole vault, hurdles, the half-mile relay and Pepe's event, the five-mile run.

Pepe could only say, "Wow! I had no idea!"

The atmosphere was infectious. Pepe was overwhelmed

with the energy, excitement, and pageantry surrounding the upcoming track competition; his nervous stomach caught him by surprise. Pepe leaned over and puked.

Coach laughed and slapped him on the back. "Good! Get all that shit out of your system. You are about to become a track star."

Pepe leaned over and again puked.

The other team had twelve seniors competing in the five-mile race. Pepe was the only five-mile long-distance runner on his team. "Coach! This is not going to work. There are twelve of them and only one of me."

Coach Harris put his arm around Pepe's shoulder. "You don't have to beat all twelve of the blue shirts, just their fastest runner!"

Coach turned away, leaving Pepe to ponder, "What the hell does that mean?"

Pepe heard a familiar warm voice calling from close behind him: "Pepe! Pepe!"

He turned, surprised! "¡*Mamacita!* What are you doing here? Shouldn't you be at work?"

"Yes, I should," shrugged su madre. "Do you think I could miss my son's *primera aventura?* No! So, I took the afternoon off."

Pepe smiled and corrected his mother. "It is my first race, not my first adventure." *Su madre* often confused her Spanish and English words.

"*Lo que sea!* Whatever," replied a happy *madre*!

In all the years they had lived in the old red brick house, Pepe had never known his mother to miss a day of work or take an afternoon off.

"Go, son! Run *rápido!* Have fun," his mother cheered him on.

"And don't let anyone in front of you," added the coach.

Pepe looked at his mom anew. He saw her pride as she beamed at him. *Su madre* stood with the other parents, proudly telling all in her broken English that her son was Pepe!

Pepe moved nervously to the runners' line, awaiting the crack of the starter's pistol. In his mind, he kept repeating to himself, "Do not let anyone get in front of you!"

The starter directed all runners to their mark. Pepe took his place and leaned forward in readiness. The other runners noticed his muscular frame and long, agile body pulsating like a thoroughbred awaiting the command to bolt from the gate. They sensed that this lone gold shirt would be hard to beat.

Pepe looked straight ahead. His foot pawed at the dirt. Unbeknownst to Pepe, he had trained his entire life for this; he was ready!

The starter's gun cracked! Pepe leaped as if to go forward but instead tripped and fell to the ground. Horrified, he looked up in anguish. The runners dashed past him as he pounded the ground with his fist. He had violated Coach Harris's two rules before he even got started. Pepe lay on the ground, humiliated.

Chapter 8

Parties are no fun if you don't belong!

Earlier that morning, Pepe and su madre had argued once again about his birthday party. Pepe pleaded, "*Por favor, mamacita!* Please, mother, no party at our house!"

His mother stood firm. "My mind is made up, Pepe! You will have a seventeenth birthday party. I have invited all of your rich classmates, and the poor ones as well."

"I am the only poor kid in my class," pouted Pepe.

Maria laughed. "Poor Pepe!"

Su madre had asked their five tenants to play the music for the party. They promptly refused to play with each other. The members told Ms. Colon that she could ask any other favor and it would be done, but they would never again play with each other. "*¡Nunca!* Never! *¡Jamás!*" emphasized Teddy, the band's former leader.

Pepe's mom smiled! "Nunca?"

Teddy shook his head emphatically. "Never! Under any circumstance," he added.

La madre said, "*Lo siento.* I am sorry to hear that." She then promptly informed all five band members to pack their bags and move out by Friday.

All five, voting with their eyes, quickly agreed to play at Pepe's birthday party.

A few days before the party, *la madre* moved about the house, singing along with the songs being played on their old Vox radio while hanging decorations and wrapping little colorful green, red and white lights to the outside white picket fence. She made Pepe come from his room to dance with her as one of her favorite Jennifer Lopez songs played. Pepe made the obligatory teenager protest but to no avail; *su madre* had him in her grip. Pepe, despite his protests, secretly enjoyed these special moments with his mother.

As they danced around the room, su madre said, "Pepe, one day a beautiful girl will ask you to dance. Then you will thank your mother for these special dancing moments."

Pepe contorted his face as if he had just sucked the juice of a raw lemon! "*¡Nunca!* Never!" he protested!

Su madre laughed and said, "*¿Nunca?*"

Pepe replied, "Never!

Su madre simply looked Pepe in the eyes and smiled. Soon she released Pepe back to his studies as she continued preparations for his party.

She swept every fiber of dirt and dust from the front stoop and patio. The day before the party, she lived in the kitchen, cooking and baking. A large pot of clam and chicken paella, flavored with a tomato base, saffron, onions and garlic simmered on her cast iron stove as she wrapped the beef empanadas and baked sweet-smelling pastries. The party was to start at five pm on Friday, right after Pepe's first track meet.

Pepe was literally in pain sitting on his bed, worrying about all that could go wrong on that awful day. He groaned, "When the band bombs, we don't even own a boom box to turn on!"

****

Su madre had hung a sign from the sixth-floor window,
"*Feliz cumpleaños, Pepe,*" and from the third-floor window
a colorful, hand-painted sign hung, announcing, "Musical
entertainment by the Caribbean All Stars!"

As the students entered the patio, they saw the table
of tasty food that Pepe's mom had prepared. They quickly
greeted his mother, "*Buenas tardes, Señora Colon. Gracias
por invitarnos.*" And then they immediately ran to the food and
began to eat.

Pepe's mom laughed and said, "Enjoy yourselves."

Pepe whispered to his mother, "Impressive! I didn't
know any of the rich kids from the hills could speak Spanish.
They must have learned it just for this party."

"Pepe! Your rich friends from the hills are from Spanish-
speaking families just as you are. They speak Spanish every bit
as bad as you. If only you would hold your head up and see the
world proudly, "*¡Ay, Diós mío! ¡Tu serás mi muerte!* Oh, my
God! You will be the death of me."

"This tastes great! We never get food this good at home,"
offered one of Pepe's classmates. Pepe breathed a little easier. At
least they were enjoying the poor people's food.

His mother stood in the middle of the yard, and her heart
was warmed by the happy faces of Pepe's schoolmates. Even
Pepe had a hint of a smile on his face. Maria Colon did an *alegre*
twirl, a lively spin, her arms outstretched; her beautiful black
hair hung in the air as if chiffon crepe blown by a zephyr breeze.
There was much joy in her heart.

Soon the five tenants emerged from the apartment house
and came over to Pepe with high fives, slaps on the back and

birthday greetings! "We are very proud of you, Pepe. We hear you are an honor student, track star, and going to college."

Always polite, Pepe thanked his neighbors and then slunk away to a corner awaiting the impending disaster.

The band members got to their instruments, and the band leader announced, "We are the Caribbean All Stars! Tonight, we play together again for the first time in many years. We play in honor of our dear friend, Pepe."

All of Pepe's classmates cheered. Pepe shyly waved but thought, "Wait until you hear their noise. You won't cheer."

Chapter 9

"*¡Levántate y corre!* Stand up and run!

"*¡Levántate y corre!* Stand up and run!" As Pepe lay where he had fallen at the starting line, a voice from the crowd tore into him like a punch to the gut: "Poor Pepe! Stand up and run!"

Pepe slowly stood up with a disgusted look on his face. "I hate when she calls me poor Pepe." But he knew he had to make a decision: "Do I want all my life to be Pepe or Poor Pepe?" He kicked at the ground, stood up and threw an angry glance toward *su madre* before racing off toward the blue-shirt runners, who were far ahead of him by this time.

Pepe tossed his thick, curly black hair from his eyes and ran as if he were racing home to meet his mother, out-running the bikes, shooting past the slow cruising Uber drivers. His long legs moved in powerful, poetic strides; his arms pumped as one with the Anemoi—gods of the Four Winds. Pepe surged forward.

Finally the blue shirts came into sight. Pepe smiled; at that moment, he knew he had this. He passed all the runners at the two-mile mark. He turned his head and looked back to see the runners behind him and smiled in great confidence. Pepe's body was one with the world, and he soared like an eagle gliding from the tallest peak.

As Pepe hit the fourth mile, he began to understand the power in his body that had been building from years of running. Those long, solitary runs had built the strength, but today Pepe unlocked the confidence. He was starting to understand. He was having fun!

At the last mile-marker, Pepe was on remote control, cruising along, enjoying his new- found power. Confident, he glanced over his left shoulder to see the runners behind him. There were none! He moved his head and glanced over his right shoulder. There were still no blue shirts. A horrified expression came over Pepe's face. There were no runners behind him! Something was drastically wrong! Coach had warned him to follow the trail markers. Pepe, not sure what he should do, kept running.

His heart sank. He must have made a wrong turn somewhere…but where? Pepe began to mentally beat up on himself. "I'm a loser! All my life has been about losing. I can't even stay on a freaking trail." Pepe did not want to finish the race. He looked for a point to exit!

Chapter 10

Everyone has good and bad days—just not on our schedule!

The Caribbean All-Stars stood behind their instruments, waiting for the count-down from their leader. The crowd stood patiently on the patio, waiting for the band to play. Pepe was in the far corner with his ears covered in anticipation of the ensuing calamity.

Teddy, the band's leader, grabbed the microphone, smiled at the crowd and dramatically slapped the tambourine against his thigh four times, counting off, "*¡Uno, dos, tres, cuatro!*"

The band hit the most beautiful chord that Pepe had ever heard. The horns, guitar, piano, and percussion burst into a beautiful calypso sound. His classmates began clapping their hands and dancing the salsa on the small brick patio. Pepe could hardly believe what he was hearing and seeing. He looked toward su madre. She smiled that smug, knowing smile of a mother.

Pepe looked around. His classmates were dancing, laughing and joking in small groups, and of course stuffing themselves on the soulful cooking of *su madre*. He saw his physics teacher, Ms. Smooch; and his old fourth grade teacher, Ms. LaFleur. Over by the food table were Coach and Mr. Sanchez, who was now the high school counselor. Both were wolfing down the paella. "Wow!" was all Pepe could say.

Something serious caught Pepe's attention. Mr.

Rodriguez, president of the International Bank of America, had abruptly pulled up to the curb in front of Pepe's home. He jumped out of his new black Navigator and moved quickly toward Pepe's mother, who was standing by the white picket fence. Rodriguez looked very stern as he moved toward Maria Colon. Mr. Rodriguez's employees often joked that he looked stern even when he laughed. However, on this evening, to Pepe he looked seriously stern moving toward *su madre.*

Pepe stood up and moved to intercede! He would not let Mr. Rodriguez disrespect his mother, even if he was president of the largest bank in America.

"Maria!" Mr. Rodriguez called.

Pepe's mother turned, surprised to hear her name called out in such a powerful way. She smiled. "Hello, Juan! How nice of you to stop by!"

Pepe, stopped in his tracks, "Juan!" His mother was calling the president of an international bank by his first name?" When the two hugged in greeting, Pepe's heart almost stopped beating.

Mr. Rodriguez saw the puzzled look on Pepe's face and laughed. "I have known your mother since she came to the Valley. She has been one of the bank's most loyal customers for many years. When I was a new bank manager, your mother was my first bank loan.

Pepe looked at his mother as if to say, "What the hell?" She only shrugged her shoulder and flashed her most perfect smile.

Soon after, attorney Juan Flores and his wife, federal Judge Rosa Flores, pulled to the curb in their chauffeur-driven limo. Judge Flores called out, "Maria! OMG, is that the Caribbean All-Stars playing on your lawn? Everyone in Argentina and the Caribbean grew up listening to their music on the radio. However did you get them to play at your son's birthday party?

"I made them an offer they could not refuse," answered Pepe's mom in her best gangster English. She started laughing, that beautiful Latina soulful laugh. Pepe loved seeing her with such happiness in her heart.

The Caribbean All-Stars suddenly switched tempo, and Teddy sang out, "Meringue."
Everyone dashed to the patio area, following the beat, clapping and singing.

Attorney Flores nudged Maria's arm! "Come dance with me. I love the meringue." His wife, Judge Flores, shooed them onto the dance floor, leaving her standing alone with Pepe.

"You must be very proud of your mother, Pepe. She has worked hard over the years, building a great cleaning business and investing in this wonderful old Victorian property. Your mother was never able to finish high school, but she wanted better for you. She wanted you to be *la primera generación*, the first in her family to go to college!"

Pepe looked over at his mother, moving around the dance floor with Mr. Flores as if she were the wealthiest person "on the island!" She looked Rodriguez and the Floreses directly in the eyes! She spoke to the affluent families from the Valley as an equal. Pepe never knew she didn't go to college, never mind not finishing high school. She just seemed so smart, like she knew everything.

Pepe stood, thinking, "How could I have known? She never talked to me about these things. She should have talked with me! No?" At the song's end, Pepe could not help himself. "Señor Flores, where did you learn to dance Latino?"

Attorney Juan Flores, a senior partner in the state's largest law firm, laughed and put his arm around Pepe's shoulder! "Do you think I lived in that big house in the hills always? I grew up in a poor Hispanic-African American neighborhood in Brooklyn, near Flatbush Avenue! We were dirt poor. My father worked as an illegal in Texas for many years to help me to get a start in America. I worked in a factory for many years to support my family while I attended community college, then four-year college, and on to law school. That's where I met, my wife, Judge Flores, at Bayside Community College. We could never have gotten our college and graduate degrees without the help of Bayside Community College.

Pepe shifted uneasily, remembering his insults toward community colleges.

It seemed as if the entire Valley had dropped by Pepe's party! They all paid honor to Maria Colon, *su madre*. "I am honored to meet you, Ms. Colon, I have heard so many wonderful things about you and your son, Pepe!"

"Gracias," replied his mother.

"Holy cow!" was all that Pepe could say.

Dr. Muhammad, the superintendent of schools, stopped by Pepe's birthday party. She walked over to Pepe and hugged him. "*As-salaam Alaykum.* Happy Birthday, Pepe, and congratulations," she said.

Pepe, replied, "*Wa Alaykum as-salaam. Gracias*! You know my name?"

She smiled. "Everyone knows your name, Pepe. You are one of the Valley's most accomplished students. I received word today that you have been selected to the National Honor Society. We are especially proud that Columbia University has offered you early admission.

Pepe could hardly breathe! This was far too much information to take in at once. His number-one school, Columbia University, was offering him early admission. Pepe instantly started to worry if he had the proper documentation that Columbia would request? If he did not, would Columbia rescind their offer? Before he could worry too deeply, *su madre* came over and asked Pepe if she might have a dance with her *hijo*.

Pepe exhaled and for the moment released his worries to the world. He took his mother's hand and led her onto the patio, where the band he had hated was playing beautiful music. Where the students he had mocked as rich snobs laughed, talked, and danced as if one big family. This all framed behind the old Victorian building that Pepe had thought worthless, *la casa de pobreza*.

Pepe's mother, laughing and smiling, whirled him around the dance floor as if she were Beyoncé and he the entertainer formerly known as Prince. He had never seen her so happy.

"Sooo, Pepe, are you enjoying your terrible party. Have the Caribbean All-Stars embarrassed you?" teased *su madre*.

Pepe laughed, "Ah, you got jokes, huh?"

At the moment the band changed tempo and began playing an oldie but goodie Trinidad Lopez favorite.

Pepe's mother turned as she felt a light tap on her shoulder. "*Perdón, Ms. Colon, me llamo Julia Melendez.* Excuse me! I am in Pepe's class. May I have this dance with your son?"

****

Pepe turned the bend, and he could see his teammates, Coach, and his mother jumping up and down and waving their arms as if warning him he had made the wrong turn. Pepe did not know what to do, so he kept running, only faster. Pepe got closer, and he realized that Coach was waving his arms frantically for Pepe to keep running toward him. A white ribbon stretched across the finish line.

"Unbelievable," thought Pepe.

Pepe broke through the ribbon, his arms raised in a sign of victory. His classmates ran onto the track, clapping and cheering, but Pepe heard only one voice in the loud, friendly crowd.

"Pepe! Pepe! You won your *aventura*! You are a winner!" shouted his mother.

Those were beautiful words to his ears and heart! It was another three minutes before the other team emerged around the bend toward the finish line. Pepe had broken the school record for the fastest five miles ever recorded.

His teammates and Coach all hugged and embraced Pepe. Pepe looked into the caring faces of his classmates. They welcomed him as one with them. Pepe's eyes watered. It was the exhilaration of belonging. Pepe would talk about that first track meet as the beginning of his understanding of wealth as being the sensation of feeling valued.

After the track meet, Pepe, along with his classmates, walked toward his home and the party. As they came around the corner, he could see his old red brick six-family home wrapped in colorful lights. Pepe had to admit it looked pretty good.

Chapter 11

No worries—you are the most handsome boy…

Ms. Colon glanced at Pepe; a mischievous smile played across her face. "Of course," answered Ms. Colon. She handed Pepe's hand to the young lady.

"*Gracias*, Ms. Colon," said Julia.

Pepe had crushed on Julia from the corners of his eyes since kindergarten. In the early years, when he rode the bus, it was Julia who always came to the back of the bus to sit next to him. She did not try to make him speak. She would sit quietly, reading a book. Pepe pretended not to notice her. Yet he would slip a peek in her direction when he thought she was not looking. But she was looking.

During school, Pepe secretly always found excuses to be near Julia. Whenever assignments required a partner, it seemed he and Julia were it. Still, he never looked her directly in the eyes or asked her out, or if he might carry her books in the hall. Julia seldom said a word. She just always seemed to be there.

Pepe took Julia in his arms, "I am surprised you asked me to dance; you are the most beautiful girl in our school."

Julia smiled and shrugged, "No worries! You are the most handsome boy in our school!"

Pepe turned a bright crimson and stumbled slightly. Julia pulled him closer as if to steady him. Pepe looked directly into her eyes and pulled her yet closer, as if to say, "I've got this!"

As he pulled her closer, her skin was soft to his touch, and he could smell the lingering fragrance of her vanilla and coconut shampoo. She wore a beautiful red carnation pinned behind her right ear. Julia rested her head on Pepe's shoulder and followed his lead. If nothing else happened good for the rest of his life, Pepe thought this one moment would carry him happily to his grave.

Su madre turned to Judge Rosa Flores, "Uh-oh! Poor Pepe!" They both laughed that "all-knowing" parent's laugh!

Chapter 12

Looking pain in the eye!

The party cleared out about midnight. A peaceful quiet had settled over the Valley. Pepe helped *su madre* clear the food and plates from the tables. They picked up party streamers and napkins from the ground and swept the party debris away.

"I am exhausted." *Su madre* sat down on the stoop. "Pepe, come sit with me."
A warm-cool wind blew in from the ocean; the black night sky was lit by thousands of tiny stars. Mother and son sat side by side, enjoying the late evening. *Su madre* took Pepe's hand into her hand.

"Pepe, I would like to talk with you." It started innocently enough, but it was to be a long, emotional night. Pepe and *su madre* sat on the stoop of their old red brick Victorian and had their first heart-to-heart talk about those dark family secrets. The conversation where the parent amidst tears and pained heart confesses to the shames and guilts too long held in that lonely heart-shaped vault.

Su madre talked of being a young girl traveling alone with the caravans over thousands of dangerous miles from Guatemala. Pepe learned that his mother was one of the undocumented. He had thought this was the case, but *su madre* would never speak of her status.

"Pepe, let me talk to you of your father!"
Pepe froze! All his life those were the words he'd wanted

to hear from his mother. On this night, an involuntary shudder made him apprehensive of what was to come.

She had never before talked of his father. It had been off limits as a conversation topic. Pepe had always been curious about his father, but the few times he brought up the subject his mother would become angry, or silent, and he soon learned it was a non-conversation. It would leave him feeling an unexplained emptiness. He later learned that it was the same emptiness felt by many fatherless boys, most of whom never come to understand the root of their emptiness, loneliness and anger.

Sometimes Pepe would cry late at night, not heavy tears but brief-moment tears, the ones that leave as quickly as they appear.

Pepe often felt that flicker of jealousy as he saw other kids holding their dads' hands, enjoying a banana split at Carlos's Ice Cream Shop or playing catch at the Little League field.

Tonight, Pepe sat motionless as his mother offered to discuss his father. An unease came over him. Perhaps he no longer wanted to hear about his father.

His mother told Pepe about her long journey across Central America . When she talked of his father, she sobbed and spoke in short sentences, seeming to gasp for air with each spoken word. She spoke almost as if she were pleading for Pepe's forgiveness.

"I was alone, Pepe! A girl of fourteen. I did not understand things. I was forced by an older man. I became pregnant."

Su madre gasped and then exhaled almost as if a boulder had been lifted from her chest, the weight of dead life lifted from her soul. She finally had said in words what she had been unable to speak since she was a child of fourteen. "I was raped!

"But from that shame came you, Pepe! *¡Mi razón para vivir!* My reason for living."

Pepe squeezed *su madre's* hand as if he would never let it go! Pepe cried! *Su madre* cried and asked for his forgiveness.

Pepe held her tightly, "*No hay necesidad de perdonar. Te amo.* There is no need to forgive. I love you!" He knew his mother had done her best, but he had never known how deep her pain and grief.

She rode the bus to and from work every day because she knew when it came time for Pepe to go to college, she would pay it, no matter the cost. Over the years, she stayed in the shadows just below the surface of Main Street America. She kept money under the mattress, and stuffed a large black plastic bag in the top left kitchen cupboard. The plastic bag was there to again escape into the night on a moment's notice. She feared banks and credit cards and anything that required an application because then they could find her. She purchased their red brick Victorian building as her one act of defiance, but she also had the guidance of Mr. Rodriguez. For years she awoke fearing that it was today that they would again come for her and snatch Pepe from her arms.

****

It had happened many years ago in El Paso, only several months after Pepe was born. Maria Colon was walking home with baby Pepe in her arms. It was just before dark, and the street lights blinked on. Maria sensed a movement from behind her before seeing a figure moving quickly toward her. She began to run, but running with a baby in hand was very difficult. The shadowy figure got closer.

Maria called out, "What do you want? Please leave me alone."

The man answered with those chilling words, "ICE! Immigration Customs Enforcement. Stop!" He held out a badge for Maria to see, but she kept moving. The agent reached for her but instead almost knocked the baby from her hands. The agent, realizing he might hurt the baby, released his grip on the child while trying to hold onto Maria. They both tripped and fell to the ground, but Maria held tightly to Pepe.

Without warning, a young man emerged from seemingly nowhere and tried to stop the ICE officer from assaulting Maria Colon. As the agent attempted to stand up, the young man grabbed him by the collar and pulled him away from Maria. The ICE agent again lost his balance and fell to the ground. The young man knew he was now in serious trouble; he had physically assaulted a federal officer.

The agent reached for his gun and tried to point it at the young man, yelling, "You're under arrest!"

The young man kicked the gun from the agent's hand and grabbed it. Pointing the gun at the agent, he yelled, "Don't move!" The young man knew there was no pulling back from this point forward. He was in serious trouble. If arrested, he would be thrown out of law school and definitely deported, his life ruined! The young law student tried to pull Maria to her feet, but she resisted. He yelled at her, "*¡Levántate y corre!* Get up and run!" Maria stood and ran! "Run and don't stop," he yelled after her. The young man threw the gun in the bushes, and he too ran.

Maria Colon glanced at the man before running off; he looked like the neighbor from her apartment building, but she was not sure. Maria raced to her apartment; her hands were shaking as she attempted to place the key in the lock. Once inside, she began throwing useless items into a large black plastic bag. She refused to turn on the lights, making packing all the more difficult. The baby sensed his mother's despair and began to cry. Maria tried to shush the baby into silence fearing he could be heard from the street.

Fifteen minutes later, Maria Colon dashed from her apartment into the night streets of El Paso, a black plastic bag in one hand and the baby in the other. It was the third time she had had to run under cover of darkness. It was the third time she had no idea where she was running.

Maria Colon for months wandered the streets of El Paso, eating at food pantries, sleeping in homeless shelters when a bed was available. Sometimes she slept on the corner steps of a local church, St. Rita, the Patron Saint of Loneliness. One day Father Castillo was bounding up the twenty stairs that led from the street to the main doors of St. Rita's. On the last step, he heard the crying of a baby and glanced to his left. A small heap from the far corner of the stairwell caught his eye. If not for the cry of the baby he would have run past the heap, assuming it was the littering of street people. On closer inspection, he realized it was a young girl with a recently born child.

Father Castillo took Maria and the small baby into the church, fed them, and gave them warm clothing. He gave Maria a place to sleep in exchange for her helping around the church, but he knew she would soon have to leave. He already had a run-in with ICE twice that year. That day came all too quickly for Maria Colon. Father Castillo gave her $20 and a bus ticket to a place called the Valley. He gave her the name of a family looking for a housekeeper. He assured Maria that this family was not picky as to whether their housekeeper was documented.

Maria Colon, at the age of fifteen, with baby Pepe boarded a Greyhound bus headed for the affluent community called the Valley.

Chapter 13

The sun will not shine where there is shade!

Many years later, one evening, Maria had just put Pepe to bed when there was a knock at her door. Maria froze! No one ever came to her house. She was afraid to answer the door, but the knocking continued. Maria reluctantly opened the door.

"Excuse me, Ms. Colon, for the interruption. I am attorney Juan Flores, and this is my wife, Rosa Flores. She is an attorney as well."

Maria could feel her body starting to tremble. She steadied herself by holding on to the doorknob of the partially opened door.

Rosa Flores continued. "We live a few miles from here. We pass your home every day on the way to work."

"What do you want?" Maria blurted out.

"Please let us in. We have important information to share with you," implored Juan Flores.

Maria, against her better judgment, let the man and wife into her living room. The Floreses took a seat without invitation.

"What is it that you want to tell me?" Maria asked again.

"We come in friendship," said Juan Flores. "My wife and I know that you are in a difficult situation with immigration."

Maria's eyes teared. She had no idea who these people were, nor where this conversation was going. It could not be good.

The man continued. "You cannot go on living this way. You must come out of the shadows to make a better life for you and your son, Pepe. We can help you!"

"You want me to turn myself in to immigration?" Maria asked in a stunned voice. Before she could say another word, Maria realized the man had mentioned her son by name. Maria exploded. "How do you know my son's name?" She could contain her fear and anger no longer. "You do not know me. I don't know you. You are just a rich lawyer from the hills. You and your wife… are you agents for the government? No? I do not know you," proclaimed Maria. "Please leave my home."

The attorney and his wife stood to leave, but Juan Flores turned to Maria. "You do know me. We lived in the same apartment building in El Paso. I caught the bus every day outside of our apartment to go to law school."

A hint of memory played on Maria's face

"I am the man who helped you to your feet many years ago when the ICE agent knocked you down. I was the one who said, "¡Corre y no pares! Run and do not stop!"

Maria gasped! The horror of that night flooded back from lost memory. She had tried for many years to forget that it had ever happened. Maria's one regret as she ran that night was that she never got to thank the young man who helped her.

Maria stood and reached toward Juan Flores. She hugged him deeply. "I have prayed that one day I might thank you. *Gracias de la profundidad de mi corazon.* Thank you from the depth of my heart."

Maria and the Floreses sat back down, this time around the kitchen table. She offered the Floreses tea and then listened for hours as Juan and Rosa Flores talked in hushed tones about the steps she must take to become a citizen.

"This is overwhelming," Maria, exclaimed. "This is too much to ask of one person."

"It is the only way," said Ms. Flores, "unless you first want to go back to your country and start new immigration paperwork from there. It is a lot to ask, but you will not be alone. We will be here for you, and families in the Valley have pledged their support. There are many others in your situation. You will not be alone."

Most families in the Valley knew the dangers faced by the Colons because each had a brother, sister, or other family member who dwelled in the shadows, Americans in every way except citizenship. The Valley over the years quietly wrapped its arm of protection around Pepe and Maria Colon! Pepe just didn't know! How could he have known?

Chapter 14

Let me relieve you of your burden…

"*¡Mamacita!* I feel so much shame for all the years I held my head down and grumbled because I had to meet you at the bus stop. I was embarrassed by you, our house, our poverty!" Pepe looked into his mother's eyes, "*¡Lo siento!* I am so very sorry, mother! I just didn't understand!" *Su madre* hugged Pepe warmly. Their forgiveness met and merged as love.

Maria Colon said, "I also did not understand. I did not understand how to tell you these things. I was so young, alone, frightened and yes, ashamed. I only wanted to do what was best for you, but I too did not understand."

The following Monday, Pepe raced home from school, running faster than he had ever run before. He sat on the stoop in front of his red brick Victorian, waving to the Valley's rich people as they drove by. They returned his wave and beeped their horns! Pepe smiled. Soon the bus carrying his mother pulled to a stop across the street. As she had for many years, she looked toward Pepe with a big smile. Waving, she called out, "Pepe, my love, I'm home."

Pepe jumped from his stoop and ran across the street. "*Mami,* let me relieve you of your burden." *Su madre* smiled, a big Maria Colon smile! She and Pepe crossed the street side by side, carrying the cleaning equipment, sprays, scrapers, rags and odds and ends that she had used to make her and Pepe wealthy.

They entered the old Victorian, laughing as they heard

the banging, clanging, and discords of the Caribbean All Stars practicing alone in their apartments.

Pepe left for Columbia that fall. Julia elected to attend the University of Barcelona, in Spain! Poor Pepe!

Epilogue

You cannot obtain wealth or success unless
someone else has suffered!
-MMS

Pepe, during his high school senior year, won the state cross-country championship title and graduated as class valedictorian. He was invited to run in the International High School Olympics, where he ran the fastest five miles ever recorded. His record stands today.

Pepe was invited to the Olympic trials by *el Comité Olímpico de Guatemala*, the birthplace of his mother, and by the United States Olympic Committee, the country of Pepe and *su madre*. He declined the invitations from both countries.

The town still raves about Pepe's seventeenth birthday as the best Valley party, ever! Somehow every family living in the Valley claims to have been at Pepe's birthday party.

After years of living in the shadows, Maria Colon emerged victoriously. *La madre* received her American citizenship in a ceremony attended by Pepe and attorney Juan Flores, and presided over by federal Judge Rosa Flores.

Four years later, Pepe graduated with high honors from Columbia University and went on to law school. Maria Colon, *su madre*, passed away shortly after Pepe earned his law degree. Maria was forty years of age.

Today Pepe, a successful trial litigator, lives in an urban community 25 miles north of the Valley. He married Julia, his first, last and only high school sweetheart. Saturday mornings they walk their kids past the bodegas, street markets and fast motions of city life on El Paseo Blvd to volunteer at the community garden. Julia still smells of vanilla and coconut and often wears a red carnation behind her right ear.

On Sundays, Pepe and Julia worship at a church that includes people both rich and poor and of all races, cultures, and orientations. After services, Pepe and his family stroll to the community center that Pepe helped build, called *Casa de Su Madre*. Inside the community center is a room very special to Pepe. It is called "Poor Pepe's Room." It is where Pepe mentors undocumented children, many of whom have self-esteem issues. He encourages them not to be a "poor Pepe" but to take pride in their heritage, and honor the suffering and struggles of their parents and ancestors."

Attorney Colon ends every class with two simple sentences, "Hold your head high! You come from a beautiful and noble people!"

It took him a long time, but he finally learned to believe in himself! He is "poor Pepe" no longer!

****